# THE PAPER PROFESSOR
# AND OTHER STORIES

## A. L. YOUNG

Copyright © 2023 by A. L. Young

ISBN: 979-8-9880030-3-8

All rights reserved.

No part of this book may be reproduced in any form or by any electronic or mechanical means, including information storage and retrieval systems, without written permission from the author, except for the use of brief quotations in a book review.

*For my Family*

# About the Book

This book contains subject matter that may be uncomfortable to some readers including but not limited to death of a parent, cancer diagnosis, divorce and dementia. Those sensitive to such subject matter should proceed with caution.

# The Paper Professor

I

The Professor had a predicament that is difficult to explain. Three days ago his hair changed from strands of red keratin to thin strips of red paper. Two days ago his nails became fragile half-circles of cellophane. Professor Milton Horace could conceal these changes under a hat or in a pair of gloves but these days it tended to damage his new hair and nails. His hair became a pulpy-wadded mess under the waterfall of rain yesterday and his nails had melted and curled inward as if his cell phone overheated. They always grew back at an alarming rate in the same pristine way and despite any prior damage that occurred. These changes were not painful but they were irksome to hide. Each new transformation brought with it an anxiety that sat uncomfortably in his chest. Horace was not sure that Miranda had noticed. It made no difference to her if he slept in a hat as they no longer slept in the same bed. Neither did it matter what his hands felt like because she did not let him touch her. Amelia was observant ever since she was a child she quickly make a mental map of her environment.

Moving to New York City at ten had inhibited her exploration. She rode the subway with the other little New Yorkers using her green student Metrocard.

***

Footsteps echoed down the corridor to his office. Amelia again. Horace snapped shut the Tupperware for this three-bean and sundried red pepper salad. The smell of garlic had already melted into his hands and the essays he planned to grade. The professor pointedly eyed the door, settled further into his chair and waited. She no longer knocked, so the door opened as soon as her footsteps ceased. In the doorframe stood Amelia; her green, bronze-rimmed eyes appeared lighter in the rays of sunlight. Her lopsided violet hair framed her face. Splotches of paint in various colors and degrees of thickness covered her clunky black boots. Her legs were so thin in comparison they looked like they would snap like crisp bean pods. She said nothing before plopping down in the black wood chair before her father's desk. Amelia rummaged through her shoulder bag that was also covered in dry paint, and took out a partially crumpled piece of paper. There was nothing neat about the girl. The professor pushed aside his lunch and held out his hand for her paper.

It was covered in red marks, none of them his and small drawing in the margins to indicate what she was trying to convey. In the upper right corner on the first page was a small old-fashioned television set with knobs, followed by a plus sign and then an equal sign all equating to a detailed drawing of a brain. On the bottom of the same page, floating on the footnotes were stick figures clutching one another's ball-like hands and also clasped between the joined hands was a paintbrush.

. . .

"What does any of this mean?" The Horace said, his voice feathery with exhaustion.

"It's about how television feeds our minds but art nourishes our connection to one another," Amelia said.

"Is not television art?" The Horace said.

"It's a formulaic art, therefore limited. It is difficult for people to show their creative work through this medium because it is for money and not all art is seen as profitable," Amelia said. Amelia talked "a great deal of nothing"(Act 1, Scene 1, pg.5)[1].

The professor read the essay once, and then a second time. The words seemed to float on the page. Many lines were crossed out with violet ink, leaving few survivors, and many words were pushed into the margins with arrows pointing to the next group of words to be read. It was dizzying and irritating to read, a kind of visual mental torture.

Their cat Benny blinked a few times before stretching his body out, scratching the essays with his outstretched hind paws. Amelia slapped her hands on her laps and Benny obliged, pouncing off the desk and onto her lap.

"The paper is not there yet," Horace said.

"Hm," Amelia appeared to deeply consider his words, edging her teeth over her bottom lip. She stroked Benny and he purred, swatting her with his striped tail.

. . .

"I wrote the first draft three weeks ago, and then I came here. I worked on the second draft for days after, and then came here. And now a third time," Amelia said.

"Another try should help," Horace said.

Amelia lowered her head, her violet hair shrouding the left side of her face. Benny suddenly sat up, his head bobbing up and down like a preying snake before bolting across the office, seeming to attack an invisible prey. Amelia stood and wiped the stray hairs from her green floral dress.

Horace leaned forward and said, "I look forward to seeing the final draft."

Amelia replied "Nice hat."

## II

It was faint, but he could read clearly the serif font word across his cellophane nails. They were slightly curled due to the heat reflected from the windowpanes. May was slowly encroaching over Brooklyn, but August heat had already smothered the narrow streets. The words in a deep onyx read imagination. The Professor rubbed the nail of his index finger. Neither the vigorous rubbing nor the oils from his fingertips could erase the imagination. Now words were coming off essays and onto him. He was wearing gloves when he looked over her essay but it was now plastered on his nail, as permanent it seemed as a Tattoo. Benny meowed. Hungry again. The professor had wasted ten minutes and had class in nine.

\*\*\*

The night Miranda told Horace she was divorcing him was strange in a number of ways. Horace remembered back to a few weeks before then and the new shirt and tie laid steam pressed by the dry cleaners on the bed. Miranda yelled from the bathroom adjoining their room that she made reservations at a new sushi place called Fusion on Court Street. It sounded like the sort of restaurant will there would be deconstructed sushi with all the ingredients splayed across the plate. He thought or more accurately hoped it meant she would talk with him. She seemed chipper when she told him at first and reminded him over the weeks.

On the car ride over Miranda applied deep red lipstick and readjusted her bra so her breast would peek out from the plunging neckline. Horace noticed they were seated dead center in the main dining room. The restaurant glowed with soft orange and green neon lights embedded in the wall in addition to more conventional white lights above head. Miranda ordered for Horace and herself and he was angry with how friendly she was with the waiter. Horace noticed then she carried her work purse with her. His eyes continued to drift to it as Miranda talked about movies, this new thing called a "Netflix Binge" and the décor of the restaurant. When all that remained was middle puddles of soy sauce on their places Horace thought they were done but Miranda insisted they try desserts as well. Horace had done the mental math in his head and the meal between the two of them cost nearly $73.54 with tax and gratuity. Miranda called the waiter over, sounding impatient. She touched his arm that time and Horace gripped his chopsticks tightly. She ordered matcha green tea sorbet and mochi ice cream.

He was sure he did not want either of those but her strange behavior made him want to see how it all would end. They ate their desserts and Horace was surprised by how much he enjoyed mochi once he got past the strange texture. The main dining area was fuller when she placed the thick packet of paper in front of him.

Miranda said, "I think it would be best for both of us."

Horace realized she meant herself and Amelia and not she and him and somehow knowing that was worst.

### III

A day later Horace felt less bulky than usual. The warm stale wind for the D train pushed him a few feet down the narrow platform like a paper bag. A young girl wearing juice-stained pink top, tutu, and rainbow-striped tights gazed at him. Her soft gray eyes utterly mystified him. The man with her he assumed was her father, by the matching gray eyes shielded her, perhaps thinking Horace was trying to get attention from the young girl. The train finally clattered to a stop, and the screech of metal on metal caused the girl to cover her ears with her hands.

Horace remembered fragments of when Amelia was that young and had the same wide and bewildered look in her eyes as the girl in the subway. As a child, Amelia had delicately put her hands on everything and had spent a great deal of time touching what she worked with. She would feel the smoothness of the wax crayons before she drew, contemplate for a long period of time what color paint to use, and sort and sort again any crafting pieces at her disposal. Miranda proclaimed Amelia was a genius and Horace was disturbed by how long the girl could observe and ask nothing. The only thing Horace was sure about children at age thirty-two was they needed many things and asked many questions, but Amelia spoke so little. She was like a small alien gathering data for her home planet.

One morning Amelia was off from school so she busied herself around the house. Fractured crayons were spread over the kitchen table. Amelia held a few in both hands like bouquets and slid them across the wide paper, creating jagged rainbows. She repeated her experiment at different lengths, created circles and phone-cord-like squiggles. Amelia looked up from her drawing and stared at Horace. At that time she was five, her eyes had darkened from blue to green, and her nose was no longer a small bump and had the beginnings of a defined bridge. Horace could not place her features.

***

It was not until he eased into a leather chair at the lawyer's office that Horace realized he lacked warmth. The warmth from the chair was like the prickly sensation of needles after submerging one's ice-cold hands in warm tap water. The human skin stayed around ninety-eight degrees regardless of external cold or warmth. Horace was as tepid as a forgotten coffee. The thought of examining himself the next chance he got was competing with his focus on why he was at the office. Entwined in Horace's beefy hand was his cell phone. Miranda had called multiple times in the last hour, expecting him home a few hours earlier. She called once more and Horace was now annoyed. He squeezed the side button, forcing the phone to sleep, and placed it on the outdated copies of Self magazine.

. . .

Horace refused to sign the documents just yet, not entirely sure he would still be himself if and when he decided but still convinced all they needed was time. The divorce lawyer opened the door to his office. It was the only enclosed one in the one-floor realtor agency turned law firm.

"Legal advice I can give, marriage advice I cannot. It is normal for people in the process of divorce to seek counseling." The lawyer spoke very casually, more so than he did with Horace in the past. He was getting paid soon so why bother with formalities?

"I'd like to see the documents," Horace said.

"Did no one serve you the documents?" the lawyer said, concern painting his voice.

"No, she gave them to me. Something happened to them," Horace said. The truth was he'd torn it in two once she left the bedroom. Miranda had had an affair at the beginning of their marriage. If there was anyone that should be divorcing anyone, it should be Horace.

"I'll copy it for you now," the lawyer said, looking at Horace's hat rather than his face. Sweat was forming around the tight band of the wool hat. If he took it off, he would be utterly embarrassed. His new hair was wet again.

It was nearly eight, and an indigo curtain had been drawn across the sky. The wind bleated through holes in the blue boards shrouding the construction site for a new block of condominiums. Gray stratus clouds were spread onto the sky like worn gauze. Horace couldn't help thinking about the identical eyes of the father and daughter, both like developing thunderstorms, with flecks of a shiny steel-like gray. Horace couldn't calculate the chances but still, the thought nagged at him in a way that weighted down his core. Amelia looked nothing like him nor his wife, Miranda. Amelia's serpent green eyes and white blonde hair clashed like shattered porcelain with Horace's red hair, Miranda's jet black hair, and their equally black eyes. The red hair came to mind; red hair was more recessive than blonde, and that is what made him unsure.

He walked through the light from long windows that stretched onto the sidewalk, pausing for a moment before going in.

## IV

Amelia's leg was hooked over the arm of the chair, popcorn balanced on her thigh and her hand resting under her shirt on her bare skin. Miranda sat near her with Benny between them, the bluish light from the television flickering on her face. Horace was in the study within earshot, which was more of a nook in the living room; the three-walled area had his desk and a small shelf with books about grammar and formatting. The rule was for Amelia to not disturb Horace.

"Mom, do you think that he really did that much damage or do you think she just wants more money like, how could an old laptop be worth a thousand dollars?" Amelia said.

"I don't know," Miranda said " suppose the hard drive or graphics card perhaps, but she will get her money anyway because of what he did to her car," folding Benny's ears down as she stroked his head. Benny kneaded his paws into the sofa, making small perforations.

"I don't think she'll win the cell phone bill bit, though," Amelia said.

" I don't know how you could watch such trashy television," Horace said.

"It's not trash; it's our justice system at work," Amelia said.

"It's a television show; it must be staged to some degree," Horace said as he flipped through papers.

"The stage is great," Amelia said. " It doesn't make it any less entertaining that it isn't real. Even the most peculiar situations are entertaining." Horace drew his complete attention back to his work. Amelia slid her leg from over the armrest; her foot thudded onto the carpet.

"Why does he always do this," Amelia said softly, leaning onto her mother. Miranda situated herself so she could hold Amelia against her chest. Under Miranda's thick eyelashes Horace could see a glare in his direction. Horace could not help but to be hyper critical of what Amelia and Miranda liked, or for that matter life in general. Miranda often told him she was sure after all of those years of having a Type A personality and reading book after book, the inhalation of all that old book glue had gone to his head.

### V

Pearls of diluted canary yellow, pumpkin orange, glacier gray and coral pink slid down the left wall in Amelia's room. The pumpkin skinned man was holding in his arms a blooming coral-colored bud. Entrapped inside was a gray child that grasped with both hands at the petals. Using varnish, the skin of the child appeared sickly and detached, almost translucent, while the scene around connected like veins, pumping life into each corner. Seven varieties of flowers, both open and closed, gravitated toward the center and parsed out specks of flowers bursting around the edges like collapsing galaxies.

Amelia's arm was bandaged in dry paint and the carpet below her new work stained with a long brownish blot. After spring break was over she would not be able to do any painting, so Amelia had to do as much as possible before the vision evaporated.

There was a light tap at her door before a soft creek. Amelia sat up in her bed, eyes half closed.

"Honey, we're about to leave for dinner," Miranda said as she ducked her head in, her thin black hair swaying beneath.

Amelia patted her bed and Miranda waltz over and sat on the foot of the bed.

. . .

Amelia nodded and looked to the wall and waited for Miranda's eyes to follow her own.

"Amelia," Miranda said. She glided to the piece and held both hands to her chest, the temptation to touch it very strong.

"Amelia", Miranda said, reverently.

"It's not done yet," Amelia said as she slid out of bed.

"I want to take a picture of this; I'll go get my camera," Miranda said in a flutter.

She did not hear Horace come to her door, only the low reverberating throaty growl. "What have you done?" Horace said through his teeth.

"I painted," Amelia said.

"On the wall?" Horace said.

"Yeah," Amelia said slowly.

"If we move, we'll have to paint all over this and replace that dingy carpet," Horace said, pointing to the brown mess.

"But we aren't moving," Amelia said.

. . .

Miranda returned, her Nikon strung around her neck.

"Have you seen this?" Horace said, throwing up his arms up towards the wall.

"Yes, I have. I have seen it, even if you don't," Miranda said.

"I see it; I see depreciated property values," Horace said.

"We aren't moving," Amelia said.

"Are we moving?" Amelia said.

Silence fell over Horace.

"No, we aren't," Miranda said. Horace's eyes widened.

"She makes a mess and you encourage it. She can paint on canvases. We can't remove the wall to put in a gallery," Horace said.

"You're in one of your moods," Miranda said as went to Amelia's side.

"Why are you so angry? Why do you hate me so much," Amelia said, blinking away tears from her eyes. As she fought back tears creases formed around the bridge of her nose as her mouth turned inward. There was nothing accusatory about her tone, only heavy exasperation.

. . .

A strong burning and squeeze sensation in Horace's chest caused him to pause. Horace felt as if he had swallowed a glowing charcoal briquette. He grabbed at his shirt with his gloved hands and looked as if he would rip off all the incandescent buttons. Miranda walked to him as Amelia stood perfectly still. Before Miranda could get a word out, Horace was able to compose himself.

"Are you okay?" Miranda said. He nodded. The pain was gone. The thumping in his chest was gone. His heart had turned to paper.

Miranda stood by the window, the setting sun pooling around her feet. She had on a look murderous enough to cause a sane person to slink away—everyone but Horace. Out of all the subjects Horace studied, Amelia was one he was unqualified to have an opinion on, according to Miranda's reactions.

"The girl," Horace began.

"Amelia," Miranda said.

"She is out of control."

"She's 16."

"Old enough."

. . .

"She needs to discover who she is," Miranda said.

Horace muttered something inaudible as Miranda' s teeth looked as if they gated words she would regret. Horace ran his finger under the band of his hat to wipe off the droplets of sweat. It did little good.

"Would you take off that ridiculous hat?"

"I want to know." Horace stood, stuffed his gloved hands into his pockets, his shoulders rising slowly into a shrug, and "Is she mine?" His shoulders dropped quickly and he softly huffed.

"Why are you asking this now?" Miranda's feet shifted in the puddle of sunlight.

"I thought her blonde hair was temporary," Horace said. " I thought she would start to look like you or me."

"That doesn't mean anything," Miranda said.

"Doesn't it?"

"Why do you want it to mean something?"

"I just need to know," Horace said. He paused, "You want to take her, is that it? You don't think I can take care of her?"

. . .

"This isn't about money," Miranda said.

"I didn't say it was."

"Let me finish, " Miranda said, " You don't seem to like Amelia. Over the last two year, she's become the girl."

"I can't help the way I feel,your's" Horace said. " I'm not the one at fault here."

"Whose fault is it?" Miranda said "Amelia's or mine?"

Horace shifted his eyes to the window, unsure of what to say. Tears slid down Miranda's face.

"We'd been in here all day dividing up blame,"
 Horace said. I don't want to get caught up in that. It's not Amelia's fault. I know that."

"You treat her like it's her fault," Miranda said. You have no idea how much it hurts me."

"It wasn't even a month."

"It was a mistake, but yours. I'm sure of it."

. . .

"Scientifically?" Horace said. "Or is it a gut feeling?"

Miranda didn't respond.

"I want a DNA test," Horace said flatly.

Miranda didn't respond.

## VI

It felt like having a greeting card in a pocket, only the pocket was unopenable flesh. His newly transformed heart was irritating and he found himself wanting his lungs and the remaining muscle to transform. Maybe then it would no longer be irritating, he thought. Horace took a Bayer aspirin to appease Miranda before she went to bed, and Amelia was watching television in the living room. A small stack of paper sat before him. In large block letters: FILED. The next page: FAMILY DIVISION. It had been signed by Miranda March. A blur of blonde fur shot across before hitting the table leg. Benny stood on his hind legs, with his front paws on the seat of the chair. Horace patted his lap and Benny scampered across the chair and onto his lap. Maybe he'd get to keep the cat in the divorce.

That'd only be if he were himself long enough. It had been nearly a week and four things had changed. His hair was red thin strips of construction paper; his nails fragile cellophane, his heart a thick cardstock and, his body lighter, how long before he was immobile and more terrifyingly nonhuman.

. . .

Amelia walked in with an empty glass and headed for the fridge before freezing in place. "Hello, Amelia," Horace said.

Amelia features' became a collage of confusion and sadness.

"I'm sorry," Horace begun.

"What is happening to your face?" Amelia interrupted. Horace touched his face and was greeted by a flat woven texture. He was able to feel the fine fibers in this new skin, finer yet stronger than his other attributes.

"You're so pale," Amelia said, her fingers shakily grazing the fabric of her loose-fitting salmon pink sweater. Amelia gripped her glass tighter, perhaps out of fear or to keep it from falling, maybe a mix of both. Neither of them said anything for a while. Horace upturned the corners of the paperwork, the sound comforting while Amelia stared. Her personality made her nearly incapable of her actions causing offense. Amelia's smooth and round baby-like face gently studied his.

"How?" Amelia said.

"I've changed," Horace said, laughing nervously, He had never been good at humor or even understanding it. He flicked the upturned corners with his fingers.

"It's been happening for about six days."

. . .

"It's why you've been acting strange, isn't it?" Amelia said. "Wearing hats and gloves in this heat?"

He turned over the documents," Yes, this is why among many other reasons."

## VII

Once the shock had subsided Amelia felt compelled to touch Horace's skin. It was smooth, raised like veins in other places that resembled dried plant fibers, yet it was warm and elastic like human skin. Amelia, like many artists, had an obsession with paper and ink. For her last Birthday, Miranda had purchased a few sheets of paper for her, the grand total being thirty-two dollars. Even that paper could not replicate the quality Horace's skin now had. Amelia wondered if she drew on it would Horace be able to wash it off. She did not ask, but the urge gripped her heart.

"You're not disconcerted with me," Horace said.

"No," Amelia said.

Horace said no more as Amelia's soft hands went over his noise that lost its roundness is was more like a halved pyramid.

A heavy guilt had risen in his flattened heart. Horace was not able to accept Amelia like Amelia accepted him because she was a creation of Miranda's selfishness. Horace knew Amelia simply accepted him and a part of him wondered if he should tell her. He quickly pushed away that idea because even if it were true it was only an excuse.

"What was the painting about on your wall about?" Horace said. Amelia stopped, positioned her right hand in front of his face before letting it fall into her lap.

"It's about the birth of the person. Not merely being born but discovering who you are. You don't have to be a child to discover it. I was not born knowing what I know now but I was gray. I had the potential to sort the black from the white. I did not have art in me but the potential was around me. It's basically a colorful representation of blank slate. Kind of ironic, is it not?" Amelia paused, folded her hands in front of her.

"We are shaped by what is around us, like how mom can be scattered sometimes and grandma is that way. The world has a way of rubbing off," Amelia said.

Horace knew that all too well.

"You understand Irony?"

"I understand many things. I've learned only from the best." Amelia elbowed Horace on his arm.

They talked all night and only noticed its passing by hunger. Amelia got Horace to eat dried seaweed. He obliged and said it was tasteless and chuckled. As the sun peeked through the blinds, settling between the rows of brownstones and young oaks Horace's eyes had become black marbles. It did not affect the strength of his eyesight but rather now his eyes had no irises to follow.

## VIII

The attic was the only place Horace could stay with his predicament. When Miranda had looked around the house for him, Amelia had told her he'd went to Hunter College early. Horace had new words printed on his skin. In addition to imagination, were divorce, custody, depreciated, and trash. Thankfully, divorce was in a place Amelia could not see. When she returned from her early college class, she had a stack of art books. Some of the Art books were pushing the corners of her backpack too far out revealing the threat that kept it together.

The attic was empty with the exception of a vacuum cleaner, boxes of Christmas decorations, and a wrought-iron canopy bed from Amelia's princess days. When she walked in Horace sat in the center of the bed, his marble eyes appearing attentive but she could not tell. She had five classes that day and much had changed. His paper skin was joined in two halves by a blanket-stitch and paper-bag-brown. His body was flatter and like that of a gingerbread man but he was still able to maintain his posture. All of his fingers were gone and only his thumb remained, the rest of his hand rounded out like a mitten. The most unsettling difference was that his mouth was gone and replaced by a large stitched X.

"I think I can help," Amelia said, speaking softer than usual.

. . .

Horace bent his head forward and back, no longer being able to nod due to lacking his longer neck. It was simply a juncture rather than a body part.

Amelia walked backward into the bed, dropping the backpack by dipping back and letting it slide off. Horace watched as she dropped the landscaped-oriented, coffee-table-sized and, oversized art books on the bed, one by one, each with a thud. Amelia discarded her backpack like it had betrayed her and quickly opened the Humanist to Post-Impressionist era art book, placing Horace's new hand on it as if he were swearing in a court of law. Nothing happened. Amelia continued to optimistically flip through the heavy glossy pages. Monet only made the colors on Horace richer but it didn't change him back to a human. Van Gogh gave him evenly segmented texture as if someone had drawn many brown dashes of varying shades but caused no other result. After three books, there was one large book of photography left. Horace patted it with his hand and Amelia took it to mean he wanted her to try.

In a strong ray of light stood a man taking a photograph of himself in front of a mirror. Nothing appeared to happen. The next photo in full color was a girl, with cotton candy blue and sea foam green hair. The stitches began to disappear, the skin rejoined front to back without an edge. The next photo was of a new baby, nude in a basket, and Horace's skin softened like the newborn. The black marble eyes remained after more than half the book before changing. Amelia smiled as tears formed in her eyes. Horace touched his face, there was a new youthfulness to it, but it was back to human. The only differences were one part of his red hair was cotton candy blue and sea foam green, and his blue eyes were now a swirl of closely packed blue dashes like Van Gogh's starry night. It was the price. Amelia could feel the warmth from his skin when their hands collided on the page.

IX

. . .

Amelia and Horace waited to hear the car roll down the driveway and onto the street before walking down from the attic. She held her backpack to her chest like a child as she walked down from the ladder. There was a strong silence throughout the house, but it conjured a warm comfort, mitigating some of the remaining unease of possible failure of changing Horace for good. They both walked down the four steps to the kitchen hungry. Horace cooked spaghetti, the only meal he could make. The twenty dollars and Wing Hua menu Miranda had left on the counter he ignored. Neither of them spoke for a while and only worked in perfect synchrony setting the table.

X

Miranda returned with a 10-pound bag of food for Benny from Beastly Bites. Horace pretended to be deep in work at his study, enclosed by his invisible wall. Amelia was sitting on the couch when she came in.

"Mom," Amelia called.

"Yes, honey," Miranda said, sounding tired.

"Can we talk?"

"Give me a moment," Miranda said quickly before putting the bag of food on the small table beside the front door, nearly knocking over the key bowl. She walked briskly into the living room and sat beside Amelia.

. . .

"Yes?" Miranda said.

"We did a makeover of sorts," Amelia said.

"Makeover?" Miranda said. Amelia nodded.

"Well, let me see," Miranda said.

Horace shifted in his seat before pushing it back a bit and standing up. Miranda looked on intently as he turned around. Miranda suppressed laughter. His hair looked ridiculous. Amelia felt something familiar but could not put her finger on it.

"It's art," Amelia said, her voice rising.

"It is art," Miranda said. The tone was not in agreement but only parroting what Amelia had said.

"He transformed because I showed him pictures," Amelia said, the words tumbling out her mouth like acrobats.

Miranda took a short intake of air, forming a vowel before stopping cold. Horace noticed her eyes more focused on him than before the divorce was filed. His eyes were like waves. It was like his eyes were in a constant spin cycle. Miranda had avoided them these past eight months but was now intrigued yet mournful that she had lost something else. Horace's eyes shifted, noticing Miranda's shifting to what appeared to be a mix of shame and embarrassment.

. . .

"Amelia and I worked on this together and I hope you don't mind the change," Horace said. Miranda's eyebrows raised, reading in his face the sincerity and reverence in his voice. This was and was not the professor, husband and dad she had known and it both made her happy and unsure at the same time. Amelia sat with her hands in her lap and still, not wanting to break the bubble of time they were in. Horace looked over to Amelia and smiled.

[1] Shakespeare, William, Merchant of Venice

# The Body Shop

The leg was now useless, and if he were going to get any decent money for it, he would have to go to the body shop immediately. He flipped through the catalog on the Formica kitchen island, trying to figure out what he could trade for it. He didn't need a new fridge; he replaced that not even a year ago. And a toaster oven was frivolous as he had an entirely new stainless-steel toaster his mother-in-law sent him from Athens, Ohio. Nancy was the manager at a home goods store and got good discounts. She saw something nice and would send it without warning. She started doing it more when his wife passed on.

Lars usually didn't buy anything but stuff that plugged into the wall. Appliances also made up a significant portion of the catalog. The back sections were food packages and clothing. Sometimes he'd get trail mix in bulk that would become stale though not dangerous after all the months it took him to eat through it. The clothing section of the catalog was pristine. The pages still loosely clung together from static cling. On the first page of the section was a tan sports jacket with faux leather elbow pads and on the edge of the page was a star that read "Free socks with order!". He didn't buy clothes like that anymore. He hadn't dated anyone since his wife died two years ago, but beyond that, it was getting cold, and he barely had enough time between work and his trips to the yard to buy warm clothes from the local thrift store. So, it, in the end, worked out. He'd return the leg he purchased that recently rotted for a new jacket and with the amount left over he'd save for a new matching pair.

The body shop was on the edge of town, small and falling apart. It was a repurposed cabin that looked to be plucked from the middle of the woods, poorly painted red and left to bake and puff like rice in the temperamental weather. It usually rained right after roasting all the people in Willow Hamlet. In the back was a well-kept parking lot of black asphalt. If there were a contest for the most visited place in town, the body shop would come very close to $2^{nd}$ to the supermarket. It was nice to be able to pluck a finger off if you were in dire need of something. Lars did that on four occasions, so his pinky to his pointer finger was like a banded rock formation at the Grand Canyon, a swatch of every nation decorated his left hand. The drive down was beautiful. The sun was setting behind the thick families of trees on the bare slate mountains. On the bridge were homemade signs for gently used arms and legs but Lars had learned his lesson. The last seller didn't provide any paperwork on his previous arm and nearly landed Lars in jail. He returned it to the police to prevent them from pursuing it any further. It was rough living without an arm for five months. Lars felt guilty about it for a while and hoped the guy they took the arm from wasn't missing it while he had it.

The body shop was a straightforward place; you went to the back room with one of the employees, they detached the limb and plugged it onto a stand to make sure it still had basic functioning. The stand looked more like a metal tree with prongs than a person, and sometimes there was more than one limb being tested at once. None of them were bloody of course, the keeper at the end of the limb and on the person kept all the internal glob in until they were reattached to the person with industrial grade magnets. They did move though, the legs back in forth as if doing a light jog, and the hands waved to no one and the arms flexed over and over again.

When Lars arrived, many limbs were being tested and a line around the row of catalogs that secured to the table with thin metal twine. He hoped they'd be able to get to him before they closed. The shop owner Max stood at the counter closing one of the registers in preparation. He wore a hibiscus bandana folded over a few times and turned into a headband around his head. His light blue button-down shirt had a small teak-colored coffee stain on it. Lars stood by the counter and Max not looking up from his till took out a form and a pen for Lars from under the counter. He immediately began filling out the form. There was a small diagram of a body to visually detail any damage. There was no point in lying. On the calf was a little soft spot of rot that seemed to have formed overnight. And 1 mole. It wasn't a defect, but people were sometimes picky. Max wanted stuff he could sell fast. He didn't have much room to kept limbs until the right person came around.

He finished the form and slid it back to Max who put it into a file tray next to the register he was closing.

"I will be with you in a minute,"

Max put the cash into a black zippered bag and closed and locked the register. He called over a short girl with green hair who was talking to a customer who was holding three hands. The man was foolish. You always needed pairs at the body shop. She took the bag from Max and took it to the back room.

"This is your fifth visit this week, a new record. Have anything good for me?" He took the paper out of the file tray and scanned over it.

Lars took in a sharp breath, "Not this time," he took out his booklet that detailed all his transactions, from the yard and the body shop and turned to the page for the faulty leg.

"Really, that was a lab created leg. You shouldn't have had any problems," He came from behind the counter and gestured for Lars to pull up his pant leg. The rot was there and noticeable. It was like a soft mossy pit, the center dark like tar but the edges green and glassy.

Max pressed his finger into the center of the rot "Fuck that's bad. It's dying." Max stood, and Lars shook his leg to let the pant leg fall back down.

"Does it hurt?"

"No, I didn't get the sensory upgrade, so it's a fancy peg leg," Lars flexed his leg.

"Those scientists know how to make a realistic leg. It's not alive, but it died. Ha. I'll let you trade anything you want for it. I'm gonna toss this," Max mostly muttered to himself, looking at the floorboards and then at Lar's clothed left leg.

Lars thought it was a waste. Max could scoop out the rot and fill it with whatever synthetic stuff they used. It was ugly, but it could not have been helpless. He shrugged and pulled his folded over catalog from his back pocket. He turned to page 501 and extended his arm to show Max.

"Anyone new in your life," Max chuckled.

Lars put his hand on the counter and leaned to one side, "Besides Jack Frost, no."

"I don't get many orders for clothes; most people want the latest phone. It should be in by next week. Have Libby finish your order."

Libby was the green haired girl. She wore torn jeans and had unicorn stickers on her phone case. Libby knew all the ins and outs of the store computer that only did what you told it to six times out of ten and even where to hit the monitor so that the fizzling sound would soften to a barely discernible drone. She scanned a code from a stack of laminated pages and took the catalog from Lars. A few soft clicks of the keyboard and a signature from Lars was all it took for some far-off warehouse to start packing his order of a sports jacket and complimentary size eleven socks. She printed off the order confirmation and handed it to Lars. He owed her a penny. Max said it was free but what he meant was very cheap. Any exchange of body parts had to have an exchange of money. It was how the government kept track of limbs and appendages. Lars gave Libby the semi-rusty penny that was cradled in his pocket lint. She took it and then held her hand out for his booklet.

The booklet was the only legal way to do any of this stuff. Trading parts without a book could get you behind bars for a long time. It wasn't like you killed someone, but it was close. To police officers, they practically considered you had gotten close to the dirty deed.

"W-ow, never seen a booklet this long," Libby said as she filled out the page. She stamped it with a nine-digit transaction number and the store's four-digit store number. Lars rented a cane from Max, got the balance refunded for the faulty leg put on the books for the next time he came to the shop and he was on his way.

There was still some sunlight left when Lars got into his car, but halfway home the sun had vanished, and a gibbous moon had taken its place in the sky. Tomorrow morning was a yard day, and he'd rise at 5:30 to make it there in time for the dump. They were always announced ahead of time, so there was still some competition. So, the more you went, the better chance you got to make any living selling parts. Savvy people sold and saved all the money they earned to open their own body shops, but Lars thought it was a risky venture. Brick and mortar was a luxury. All you needed for business was two people, a buyer, and a seller and well, maybe one more thing: honesty. If you always had squeaky clean parts, then people kept coming.

Lars's home was down the road from his neighbor that never said a word to him and always wore plaid pants. He was an alright neighbor. Still cleared his section of the path when it snowed. But he also always hung anti-body selling flags in his window like some suit of armor. As he drove past his neighbor's green house with white doors, he felt an itch of irritation that slithered up and clutched on to one side of his face, making his lip curl up. He sped past the house and jutted onto the curb as he was parking into his driveway.

Over his evening coffee, he took another look at the ad for his jacket. He hoped tan looked good on him. His sense of fashion was anything that still fit and wasn't stained. His wife hated when he came home from the yard covered in bodily liquids and materials. Lars would joke "the surgery was a success" and then wash with the gritty soap Maria kept in the bathroom.

The sun had already slugged up the walls before Lars stirred. His alarm didn't go off, and it was nearly 9 am. He went to the yard nonetheless, hopping into the car and throwing his cane into the backseat. Six pairs of decent arms were enough to make up for the lack of hours he had been getting lately. It would mean he could coast for the next month until business at the warehouse picked up.

The yard was next to a parking lot for school buses. There were no kids on the busses while the adults were doing their business, so no one to blame for the scaring of children unless their parents traded parts.

The dump of parts was already picked over, and then what remained were those of children and subpar adult limbs. There wasn't much of a market for rotted legs or a five-year old's arms. Most had blue tags meaning they were from a medical facility. A red tag meant lab-created, and a green tag indicated a criminal forfeited it. Those were rare. There weren't many judges that sentenced convicted people to lose an appendage, believing it outweighed the crimes—even that of murder. In the end, he managed to get a decent pair of blue-tagged arms.

On his way to the trailer that was the office of the dump, he bumped into a woman rolling a wheelbarrow of legs towards a purple flatbed truck.

"That's quite a haul," a hint of jealousy in his tone.

She looked up, startled. Her hair was greasy, and a strand clung to her weathered cheek. She wore stained acid wash overalls and brown boots. Her shirt was orange like a desert sunset. Her eyes were round and dark.

She croaked "I stood on line at 3 am," as she walked towards the truck.

. . .

The next three weeks Lars didn't see her, but he thought about her every time his mind wandered. He came a few days at 3 am and then 2 am and even still at 1 am and didn't see her standing in line. This was the case for three weeks. Women didn't come to the dump site unless their children needed a part. They weren't involved in the business, at least none that were his age. He was impressed with her. Lars had gotten lazy by arriving a 5:30. He used to come at 3 am when his wife was alive. She would start a pot of coffee when she went to the bathroom and nudged him on his side, right in his appendix. He didn't have to feed anyone else but himself, their only kid, Kate, left a year ago. He wondered if she had any kids. She had to be at least 50, maybe 60 years old. He wondered if she was married. Who did she feed with her limb money?

The jacket arrived in a beat-up box covered in transparent yellow tape with the same Chinese character repeated over and over again. The coat had a plush feel, and the exterior was impossibly smooth. His socks came later that day in a small padded envelope. The weather was beginning to turn but not cold enough to need a jacket. He haphazardly folded it up and threw it in the backseat.

On the way to the warehouse for work he picked up some coffee from a Mcdonald's drive thru. He took quick slurps at red lights and nibbled the sweaty package of blueberry muffins he found in his glove compartment. Today a shipment was coming in so it was going to be a twelve-hour minimum shift. The sun was still lightly edging the mountains in gold as he wove his way down the cracked back roads toward town. Three pallets were being lowered from the white 18-wheeler when he arrived. All the workers stood around a long card table that had a few boxes hot coffee and bagels, stuffing their faces and warming their hands in their pockets. HEELY & CO was a supplier of restaurant goods from paper cups to industrial ovens.

Lars grabbed a poppy seed bagel and some stout tiny containers of cream cheese on his way into the building. He'd love to talk but shifts were not going to discover themselves. On a large blue tinged map was all the routes and dates of shipment. The longer the distance, the bigger the shipment. For the month of October there were eight. He took out a bent notebook from his back pocket and jotted down the dates. All of them, no matter the time. There was still eighty hours to make up from this month alone.

The boss was at the very end of the building in a large office that wrapped halfway around the warehouse floor and enclosed by large glass windows. Like a prison warden he could pace back and forth from one end of his domain to the other, watching trolley after trolley of shipment be unloaded and taken to their respective shelves. Murray didn't miss anything.

After one soft rap on the door Murray rose from his wine red office chair and let Lars in with a deep, almost gritty sigh.

Heavily sliding his hands in his pockets "Good morning, Anderson," rose from his chest, loud and booming.

Lars began stroking the edges of the notebook with his fingers, "Good morning, Boss. How's the family,"

This seemed to make him happy as he floated over to his desk and picked up a picture frame, "A new addition".

The clearly homemade mosaic frame held a slightly too small picture of a big-eyed baby wrapped into a ball with a bright yellow gauze blanket. The eyes were like round black stones edged by translucent skin.

He smiled as he spoke, "Goodie was born two months ago, daughter and my son-in-law haven't slept since."

It was such an odd name for a child. Lars didn't think he'd ever hear someone say the word in any other way but sarcastically so, he smiled and said "She's precious". Lars did not care for children, or adults for that matter. The only child he ever felt a connection towards was his daughter.

"There's a few shipments of stoves coming in. Could you use a hand or two," Lars waved his rainbow hand like a flag and grinned.

"A few guys from corporate are coming and I think it's best we stick with the established schedule, can't look disorganized," He pulled out a stack of paper, eyes still trained on Lars. The board outside was covered in pen marks, indictive of last-minute changes. Lars knew what he was really saying. It was like when his daughter said she needed to "Get a breather," whenever Lars would come home with some fresh parts.

Lars looked at the center of his forehead and nodded stiffly.

"How about the 21st?"

"Sorry Lars, I'm afraid that's full,"

"Just trying to make up these 20 hours from this week. Any chance at working overtime tonight?"

"I imagine we'll be done before the shift is out,"

"Huh, I see...I see. Well, I should put on my gloves and start. It's almost arrival time,"

Lars gave the picture of Goodie on his desk one more look, "really cute kid," and left the office.

Just as Anderson said the shipment took far less time than allotted and Lar's was now short eighty-four hours. Driving back Lars read whatever billboard that glided pass him and tried to memorize the numbers. There was one for hair removal, indoor rock climbing and one that simply read #Freedom is the End, no number. Lars considered getting another job. Perhaps at the paper factory, though he heard that even those hours were hard to get. If he was going to sacrifice trading and selling, it had to be for something good enough to pay the bills on its' own.

His neighbor was sitting out on his yard when he got home, drinking something from an orange plastic cup. Parked in Lars' driveway was the purple truck of the woman with a sparkly mountain decal he didn't notice before. He could see the silhouette of her untamable hair and smell the stench of rot. In the yard it was easy to ignore but in the open, among normal surroundings it was difficult to ignore. Lars parked on the car on the curb and approached the purple truck. The woman seemed to be half asleep when he walked up to the car but when he was right at the window he saw her doing some accounting in her log book.

"How are you?" Lars said, smiling.

She turned her head slowly but Lars was still stunned by the deep black nature of her eyes. His own were wide, unable to take them in all at once. She then dug into her bag like Lars was a police officer and produced a clipboard.

"Max said you bought a lab created leg recently. Well, I have this for you to sign. You'll be number 280."

It was a petition for compensation for faulty legs. Lars at first lifted his hand to push it away, he already got his money back but then he paused. It would be like questioning a blessing which Lars didn't go to church but he guessed was most likely wrong. His budget thread thin and any potential extra money was worth his janky signature. He took the black pen from underneath the metal clip and signed his name then printed carefully his address and phone number. Scanning the page he noticed the area codes were from nearby and from counties dozens of miles away. He wondered if that's what she had been doing for close to a month.

"How's your trading been going?" She said, her voice dainty.

"I've been slacking," Lars said.

"Do you travel at all?"

"Travel? I can't afford a vacation."

She shook her head, like a parent would to a child "No, I mean to trade."

Lars hadn't considered that. From the film covering the flatbed of her truck he could tell she was far more in it.

"Where does one go?"

"What is in the budget I guess. I go five hours away a few times a month. I went to India and Thailand twice but that's only because my mom gave me her miles," She glanced at the clipboard and Lars turned it over.

"Did all those people have faulty lab created limbs?"

"Most but some just got infections, not all of them rotted the new limb itself," She said in a rush.

Lars nodded straight up and down. He didn't understand why she was doing any of what she was doing but it was more than he ever saw anyone else doing. Most people, himself included, bought or dug for their limbs, sold and traded and then went about their lives. There was no one fighting for the rights of people in the trade. Most people thought they violated the rights of other people. That's what his neighbor thought. That Lars was some kind of monster, one step to being a serial killer but, instead treading as close as the law would allow. Trading was the new abortion.

"I don't think we ever formally met,"

"Joan," she spoke into her bag, shuffling up a twisted scarf, making room for the clipboard. Lars played around with the name in his closed mouth. He wanted to say it out loud. Joan then looked up and started the car, she frowned sympathetically and said to her dashboard "I'll keep you in the loop," as she began to back out of his driveway.

"See you, Joan," Lars said far too quietly for anyone to hear.

The next day it felt as if air had filled his lungs for the first time. It began as a trickle and then a baptism of solace as he dog eared pages of the trading catalog. The sensation was deep and pulled him into himself. It was like a string had been pulled at his foot, pulling together all the separate wooden blocks, steadily and rigidly into place. He didn't know where Joan lived or worked, besides the yard and all he had to look forward to was some form of contact which most likely would not come from her but a law office. Those things could take months and he really did not want to wait months. On the way back from the supermarket Lars went to The Body Shop. Max wasn't there yet, as Fridays were his late start days but he wanted to beat the crowds and monopolize him before anyone else could. Lars stood by the catalog table and paged through each one, from page xxi to 897 and then again. The corners shifted from yellow to taupe, to lavender and then to blue to indicate the sections.

A line was forming around the catalogs and all but one register was continuously ringing when Max arrived carrying a metal latch box. Lars snaked around the table and stood in his path, Max looked right pass him and walked over to the open register on the right. Lars followed behind him, cutting in front of a teen girl with short brown hair and gold shorts holding a pair of hands under her arm.

"I thought the deal I gave was pretty decent," he spoke up into the air, as if even looking at Lars would set off a nuclear bomb. Lars's words sputtered like a little boat.

"No it was a perfect deal, a great one. It's not about you, really,"

"All I knew was Joan came in here demanding information. She had done all the paperwork so I had to give it to her and then I see that my shop ratings have dropped," he placed his hands on the counter like he was testing if it were still hot "I just wish you gave me a heads up or something, ya know...before you tried to screw me over."

Lars didn't think. He didn't think at all. If he were honest, he didn't consider the possibility that it would get back to Max.

"You ever hear of the traders' creed? Well, here's a cliff note, you don't get involved in a class action lawsuit or any lawsuit with your dealer."

"It was with the lab though. She didn't say it would be you,"

Max rolled his eyes and stomped once on the floor hard with his left foot.

"Lars, are you serious?"

"She doesn't look like she's out to get you," Lars held out his hands as if in prayer.

"She's not out to get me, she just doesn't think when she tries to crusade," Max said, slightly calmer. Lars saw his in like a big open refrigerator door in the middle of the night.

"Maybe you can give me her address and I could talk to her?"

Max softly said "Come," as he headed toward the back room. It was formally a waiting area but it had been turned into a short term storage area sectioned off by only a heavy black curtain bolted up to the rafter above.

Max scribbled out an address before Lars could even separate the drape enough to cross over.

Joan lived nearby, not even two miles from him. The neighborhood was small and mostly stout apartment buildings standing on unkept asphalt lots edged with dying grass. Every hundred feet or so were fast food restaurants, signs for parts roped on to gates and homeless people begging. Joan lived in on of the few houses on the perimeter. It was a stone house sitting on lush Bermuda grass. Lars immediately thought it couldn't possibly be her's. He walked up to the door but stopped to glanced back. He still had the crumpled jacket in the car, and the thought occurred to him he'd look less suspicious and seem less intimidating. Lars took large strides back to the car, put the jacket on and walked back down the pathway. Still unable to knock, he considered what he would say. He couldn't possibly say "I like you. I want to be around you" so he tried to think of a legitimate question about the lawsuit. He decided to ask how Max would be effected. It could be a long conversation and the thought made him happy. He knocked and moments later he could hear a dog tapping their untrimmed claws on the floor and high pitched barks. The door swung open immediately after and there Joan stood, hair clean and straightened, wearing a soft long geometric print dress and black ballet flats. She looked like a soccer mom or maybe perhaps the wife of a doctor. She looked worlds, even universes from the trade. Lars realized he was wearing his stained pants, the one with the worn out patch on the left knee and an oil stained Regan t-shirt. Joan's eyes were full of light and she moved to stand closer to the doorframe. Lars, not registering the invite backed up slightly.

Joan chirped "Come in please, I was just watching the news."

Lars didn't know what to do with the little detail she watched the Friday afternoon news but he was hungry for more little details. She had a dog, lived in a stone house and must liked purple a lot to have a purple car.

Joan took him to the kitchen and floated quickly between the cabinets, stove and refrigerator getting a snack for him. Apple slices, cubed cheese and red grapes. Lars wasn't sure of the last time he bought grapes or any fruit. His daughter, Noa loved fruit so any he bought was for her. She hadn't come over in more than a year so chicken, nearly expired milk and a hardening roll cake was all there was in there now. Joan began to talk about the lawsuit and Lars listened for a few minutes but then stopped when she realized he wasn't eating but staring down at the plate in front of him. Joan stretched her open hands out in front of her over the kitchen island and towards him. It seemed to deeply confuse him as he moved his own out of the way and looked up.

"Did you want to remove your name," Joan asked gently it seemed to have an immediate calming effect.

"No, I just wanted to talk with you," Lars said as formally as his voice would allow.

Joan continued to talk, and then got a stack of papers and explained more. Most of the words fell from his head as soon as the vibrations slowed in the air. But he continued to listen, and watch how her hair fell around her face as she spoke and take in as much as he could of her deep black eyes. In the background the news was ending and the theme was echoing off the walls and high ceilings. Just to be adjacent to her was more than his being could handle.

# THE GIRL WITH FLOWERS IN HER HAIR

Mrs. Hershel's clouded eyes were half focused on the *Price is Right* playing softly in the background on her mini-flat screen on the kitchen island. The teakettle on the stove for her morning coffee was nearly ready. Although, on Dr. Kang's orders she shouldn't be drinking, she'd read an article online about it being good for the heart. Her heart had given her trouble on a regular basis since March. She had to pause often when she went up the stairs to visit her friend Jill. All of that was the boring stuff. Once she turned off her silver teakettle, she'd make a mug of lightly sweetened coffee and go and visit Skylar. The mug she often used was teal with a raised decoration of a seashell. Skylar had brought it back from her trip to Palm Beach a few summers ago; she always brought her mugs and flowers.

A high-pitched whine reverberated from the kettle on the stove and Mrs. Hershel walked over to turn it off. Taking the mug off the pale yellow nook below the cupboard she poured the water half way and added two tablespoons of instant dark roast, having to stir often to keep it from turning into an unpalatable tar. She added four packets of *sweet-and-low* and brought it to her lips. She pursed them shut. It was not sweet enough. After two more packets, Mrs. Hershel had her coffee and went to her bedroom.

Her bedroom was bare. She'd recently moved to what her daughter called an "independent living community." On her dresser, she had a mirror, rolled out lace runner, and a jewelry box. There was also a framed picture of her late husband, Skylar, and, her daughter; Skylar's dark brown hair proofed around her head, filling most of the frame and her thin light brown arms encircling her mother's neck. There were a few other pictures, but she couldn't remember their names. Her bed was made with a generic stripe pattern of purple and blue, with four lines on each end, given to her by the caregivers. In the corner, she had a small side table with a tiny blooming cactus, also given to her by Skylar. Her only complaint was the odd mildew smell that came from the crown molding, which indicated a past flooding.

Mrs. Hershel took off her polka-dotted robe and nightgown and put on her lavender skirt suit. Then, releasing each strand of her hair from its cylindrical imprisonment she styled them. She fastened an incandescent lavender clip to her graying tresses. She slipped on a pair of white patent leather heels and called a cab. She was no longer allowed to drive. The cab driver picked her up behind the tennis courts; pass all the identical stucco houses and pool with not nearly enough water to swim in. The other people in the community liked the aquatic workout sessions offered Tuesdays' at noon.

"Where you headed?"

"This address," Mrs. Hershel said, handing him a reply envelope with Skylar's address on it.

"Oh, the Smith residence."

\*\*\*

The cab driver turned the corner and left the independent living community, stopping for a red light on Berkley Avenue and 2nd Place. The ride was devoid of conversation, and the only sound was that of police sirens and gusts of wind that rattled the windows of the old black cab. The trees were deep in slumber, stripped bare of leaves and what Skylar called *whirles*. The uneven slabs of sidewalk were blanked in snow and ice perforated by blue salt.

"That will be $36.70."

Mrs. Hershel opened her purse and handed the cab driver a fifty-dollar bill, he handed her change back over his shoulder.

"Thank You."

"No, problem. I'm sorry for your loss."

***

Mrs. Hershel did not have time to respond before he drove off and up 2nd Place. Parked in front of the house was a plain navy blue car with a police siren silently blinking on the dashboard. Mrs. Hershel walked up the hexagon-paved driveway, her heels crunching the partially melted ice and scrapping the blue salt under her worn heels. It was freezing and the tips of her fingers were becoming numb. In the corner of her eye, she could see yellow police tape across the garage. She picked up her pace and knocked on the large oak door. No one answered. She knocked again. This time the door slowly opened and her daughter stood, wearing a large heather gray cable-knit sweater, her oak-brown eyes swollen like golf balls and her curly locks greasy and tangled.

"Where is my Skylar?" Mrs. Hershel said.

The woman covered her mouth, like she would vomit at any moment and her chest rose and then fell like a brick.

"Where is my Skylar?"

The woman took her by her icy weathered hands and led her to the living room. The air was stale with mildew and mustard-like scent and dust gently floated on shafts of soft light from the window. Mrs. Hershel took her hand away in disgust.

"Where?"

"We don't know where," Her voice seemed to evaporate with each word.

"Why wasn't I told about my daughter?" Mrs. Hershel said.

"She's not your daughter, we're not your family, Mrs. Hershel,"

"That's a lie."

"She volunteered. Skylar is not your daughter, Mrs. Hershel."

Each word jabbed Mrs. Hershel in the heart. Why would this woman say such things to her?

"You're a horrible person!" Mrs. Hershel shouted.

The woman covered her ears, cuffing them tightly and shook her head as if to dislodge Mrs. Hershel's words.

"Please, listen. Skylar is missing, and I can't do this right now." Tears stained her sunken and dark cheeks.

Mrs. Hershel noticed a gangly man walking out of the kitchen, a gun in his holster and a fat black leather pad in his hand. He wore thick tortoise shell glasses, a powder blue button-up with slacks and an apologetic expression.

"Does she have any information?" he said.

"No no no, she was about to leave," The woman said as she shook her head.

"Not until you find my daughter."

"Is she?" he said.

"No, she's not." The woman said, jabbing Mrs. Hershel again in the heart.

"I want to help," Mrs. Hershel said.

The gangly man nodded, his eyes now focused hard on Mrs. Hershel. The woman gave Mrs. Hershel a hard stare.

"I am Detective Darren Darcy," He shook her hand.

"Nice to meet you, I am Mrs. Hershel. Skylar's mother."

"Have you had any contact with her on or after March 4th?" Darcy said.

"Yes, she brought me soup from a shop on 5th and 2nd place," Mrs. Hershel said.

"That's impossible, she was in school," Skylar's mom said.

"She skipped her last period," Mrs. Hershel said matter-of-factly

Detective Darcy and the woman exchanged glances. He took out his smartphone from his pocket. Within a few moments, he was on the phone with the deli and left for a moment after saying he would be back soon to the woman as he grabbed his leather jacket off the white *LazyBoy*. The woman and Mrs. Hershel were now alone in the two-story colonial and both women still stood mere feet from the door.

"There is coffee in the kitchen, you want any?" the woman said.

"Yes, dear," Mrs. Hershel said.

\*\*\*

Both women held mugs of coffee in their hand as they sat a few feet apart on the white sofa.

"When did she go missing?" Mrs. Hershel said.

"We thought after school but now we know after she saw you. She went missing on March 4th" Skylar's mom said.

"I'm sorry, what is your name again?" Mrs. Hershel said.

"Marisol,"

"Marisol. Marisol. That doesn't sound right. I thought it was Julianne," Mrs. Hershel said.

"That's your daughter's name," the woman said.

"But you are," Mrs. Hershel started but then stopped when she noticed the hardness of her eyes.

"How are you getting on there?" Marisol said.

"It's alright, I guess...I have my coffee and mugs from Skylar. My room is quite large. I have a window that has a view of the pool," Mrs. Hershel said.

"Nice," Marisol said.

"Look, I'm sorry. We will find her," Mrs. Hershel said. She placed her hand on Marisol's lap.

"I pray," Marisol said.

\*\*\*

Detective Darcy returned, his notepad in his gloved hand and his face red from the onslaught of cold air and flurries. Marisol jumped from the couch like she had been burned.

"Did you find out anything?" Marisol said.

"The cashier saw her around 3 PM, she bought soup and asked for two spoons," Detective Darcy said.

Mrs. Hershel wore a smug grin; she knew her Skylar visited her, even if people insisted on not believing her anymore.

"It fills out the timeline if she went to Oak Hill to visit Ms.–"

"Hershel," Marisol filled in.

"That means she went to Oak Hill, which would have taken her roughly thirty minutes, and visited with her. Now we proceed with the investigation from there," Detective Darcy said.

Mrs. Hershel put down the mug of half finished coffee and joined the two.

"She left around *People's Court*," Mrs. Hershel said.

"What time was that on?" Detective Darcy said.

Mrs. Hershel touched her lips.

"The sun was down," Mrs. Hershel said.

"So after four or five," Detective Darcy said slowly.

"Yes," Mrs. Hershel said. She nodded profusely, her dry and wire-like gray curls bouncing around her head.

Marisol folded her arms, looked down at her feet and tried to focus on the image of her daughter, safe and happy.

"We have to go to Oak Hill, maybe someone saw her leave," Marisol said.

Marisol and Mrs. Hershel sat in the back of the police cruiser as Detective Darcy punched in the address for Oak Hill Independent Living Community on the GPS. Mrs. Hershel was cold; she did not understand why there was snow in August. It was eighty degrees the last time she was outside. Detective Darcy backed out of the driveway, slightly skidding on the ice on the slope leading to the runoff drain. Margret made Mrs. Hershel a silver thermos of coffee for the trip back.

As Detective Darcy made his way through the white arch of the community, a group of three police cruisers had formed a barrier. He tried his best not to give away any hints that this may be a very bad sign. Skylar's mother was gripping the seatbelt.

"What's happened, Darren?" Mrs. Hershel said.

"They are helping us find your daughter," Detective Darcy said. He waved his right arm and Officer Roy walked over. Darcy rolled down his window.

"Darcy, drive up to house 12,"

Darcy nodded. After the cruisers shifted to the side and partially onto the well-manicured lawns Darcy drove to quadrant 6 and up to house 12, which faced the pool.

"Wait in the car," Detective Darcy said as he climbed out of the car and closed the door.

"Why are they at my house?" Mrs. Hershel said. Ribbons of police tape were plastered on the house, laced around the metal bars on the windows on both sides of the front on the house and obstructing the front door.

"My guess is looking for clues, you helped us a lot," Marisol said.

"Why are they at my house?" Mrs. Hershel said, sounding angrier.

Margret clasped her hands together and sat them in her lap.

Detective Darcy ducked under the police tape and knocked on the door before being let in by another uniformed police officer.

A moment later Detective Darcy returned, this time opening the door on Marisol's side.

"Please come with me, there is something you have to see," Detective Darcy said.

Marisol paused for a moment, her face blank.

"Come," Detective Darcy said.

Marisol walked in with Darcy, her arms tightly crossed and the wind wiping around the back of her heather gray sweater. The white door with the peeling paint was barely opened as they entered.

Mrs. Hershel gripped the thermos as she took a sip of the still piping hot coffee and placed it in the cup holder in between the front seats. A gust of wind rattled the windows as a sharp scream came from the house. The front door swung open, stretching the police tape as Margret began to charge towards the car, only to be held back by a dark haired police officer twice her size.

"Where is she?" Marisol screamed before crumpling over the arm of the officer nearly falling on the icy ground.

Mrs. Hershel madly shook her head.

The officer helped Marisol up and walked her back into the house.

\*\*\*

A short bouquet of pink carnations and marigolds floated in a vase of ice water on the kitchen table. On the stove simmered a thick clam chowder from the local deli. It was Mrs. Hershel's favorite. Mrs. Hershel flipped through the channels on her TV to find the news. It was difficult to find things now with cable. Half the channels were sports or networks that did not broadcast in English. Skylar didn't seem to mind the lack of TV and she hummed as she took out a pair of bowls.

"How much do you want?" Skylar said.

"Oh...about half way, have to watch my sodium," Mrs. Hershel said.

Skylar made two bowls and grabbed a pair of spoons.

"This is so kind of you dear, my daughter–," Mrs. Hershel said.

"Julianne," Skylar finished.

"Right, she doesn't come see me that often."

"I'm sure she loves you."

Mrs. Hershel nodded and skimmed the top of her chowder with the spoon.

"Still hot, we'll eat later. I got something to show you," Mrs. Hershel said.

"Sure, what is it?"

"Come, come."

Mrs. Hershel laid a large hatbox on the bed. It was ecru with a fading pink rose design with the words Love, Peace and, Family printed all over it in a thin calligraphy font. She pulled off the thin top slowly, the edges damaged and revealing the plain brown cardboard underneath. Skylar was excited. In watching how tenderly Mrs. Hershel opened the box Skylar knew it meant it was special. With her pale weathered hands, Mrs. Hershel pulled out an evergreen sweater. On the right breast was a large rose broach with incandescent petals and a green lace stem. The petals were a milky pink stained glass with metal edges and folded over one another forming a blooming bud.

"Well, come and try it on."

"Oh, it's beautiful," Skylar said.

Mrs. Hershel helped Skylar into the sweater. It was a long and hung past her hips but Mrs. Hershel was sure Skylar would grow into it. She had long arms that fit the sleeves perfectly; soon her legs would catch up.

"It looks wonderful on you Julianne," Mrs. Hershel said.

"I'm Skylar, Mrs. Hershel," Skylar said, gently. Mrs. Hershel froze for a moment before nodding, remembering again. Mrs. Hershel ran her hands over the sweater, miles away in thought. She smiled, her protruding cheekbones enveloped by concentric circles.

"I bought this for Julianne before she went away to college. She didn't like it. Never really cared for girly clothing. I thought she might need it for interviewing later down the line,"

"Are you giving this to me?" Skylar said as she touched the brooch with the tips of her brown fingers.

"Oh, yes, very much so. It's no use here and stuffed in an old hatbox."

Skylar nodded and rubbed her fingers on the cuffs, admiring the texture.

\*\*\*

Mrs. Hershel placed the reheated bowls of chowder on the lace runner of the dresser and they ate in the room with the chairs from the kitchen pushed up against it. As Skylar finished eating Mrs. Hershel combed her hair, braiding from one side of her head to the other and forming a crown. It tamed some of her curls and the taut hair formed a wavy pattern. She then used some of the pink carnations to lace through her braid and tucked the end of the braid underneath, securing it with a hairpin.

"Done," Mrs. Hershel said.

"It's like I've been transported back in time," Skylar said.

"Do you not like it?"

"No, I do. I really do. It looks just like the photo,"

Skylar picked up a black frame from her dresser. The woman had long auburn hair and pink roses laced in the braid around her hair, like a crown. The photo was not on photo paper like the others but printer paper. Upon closer inspection, she noticed the picture was pixelated. Her pupils were squares and each shade in the picture, from dark to light was grainy. In the center were thin white lines, indicating a rarely cleaned printer printed it.

"When was this taken?" Skylar said.

"I-I don't really remember," Mrs. Hershel said. Mrs. Hershel took the picture from Skylar, placing it back on the runner after smoothing the lace with her hand.

\*\*\*

Having her weathered hands through my hair felt nice and the velvety flowers softly brushed against my temples. She hummed to herself as she tidied the top of her dresser, admiring the other fancy hair combs she had and comparing some of them to my slightly darker skin. She placed a tortoiseshell comb in my hand and nodded. The shadow from the drapes stretched across the floor, daylight was quickly running out and I would have to get back by 4:50 pm the latest so my mom would not, rightly so, think I skipped class. She sat on her bed and clasped her hands in her lap, seemingly lost in thought. I just needed to tell her but I could not make myself stand. The worst part was I knew she might not even remember I told her I would never come back and she would sit at her kitchen island waiting for me. I wondered how much she would wait before she realized I was never coming back. I hoped she would remember that it was not because of her that I was not coming anymore. She got up from the bed and hugged me from behind, rubbing my shoulders and adjusting my hair a bit.

"I have something to tell you."

"You can tell me anything, Julie."

I ignored the use of Julianne's name and continued.

"I can't come back any longer."

***

Julianne burst through the bedroom door and unburdened herself of the evergreen sweater. The brooch hit the linoleum and Julianne turned back. Mrs. Hershel looked confused. Julianne tore the carnations from her hair, the fleshy stems becoming mere strings and pulp as the delicate petals whirled toward the floor.

"Please don't go, Julie," Mrs. Hershel called out.

Julie swung open the door, the soft canary yellow and cobalt blue hues of day turning into night stretched onto the floor and flurries were wisped in by freezing gust of wind. The soft glow of light from the dulled sun reflected off the soft shimmering piles of snow filling the empty space around her trembling form.

***

My fingernails were a shade of lavender and the tips of my fingers nearly red. Identifying frostbite was not a skill I had but I was sure I had it. The sweater kept me warm for a while but soon enough the ice-cold air seemed to reach every nook and cranny and prick my skin raw. I damned myself to the point I was screaming in my head about how foolish I could be to not go home and how I could not tell my mom that Mrs. Hershel was getting worst. I thought I could handle it. She would call me Skylar when I brought her clam chowder and it became an experiment to see if I could help her more. I was not sure where I was but I did not feel far enough away. I had never seen her that angry before.

The woods were dense where I was and what little daylight was left was filtered so finely through the tops of the trees the light looked like glitter. I held my knees close to me in an effort to keep warm. Eventually, someone would notice. The school would call and leave an automated message on my mom's cell phone telling her I was late for class. My shoulders faltered a little when I realized she was taking a night shift and her phone would be off for hours before she listened to any messages. My phone had not service out here, I was cold and I was sure my scalp was bleeding. I began to cry, the tears pooling into my cupped hands. Softly at first, and then more violent like a bleating lamb I heard them. *The sirens.*

# Making a Home

The green and gold urn sat in an open cardboard box, the overhanging naked branches gliding off of its shiny surface as they made their way through Manhattan. Ken drove faster, not wanting to miss the next green light. The day began early for them because they picked up her mother's ashes from the funeral home at 8 am, and would meet with the real estate agent and talk about the possibility of selling the home at 10:45. The interior rattled a little as they moved through SoHo and the sky grayed as rain began to fall. The number of street lamps became sparse as they inched beside Chelsea Pier caught in a throng of yellow and green Taxis. The nausea and fatigue began to set inside Harriet's stomach and head. The funeral had been two days ago, though Harriet easily lost track of hours. When they returned home after the funeral two days ago Harriet went to make coffee, but instead she sat at the kitchen island with her index and forefinger poised inside the cup and looking out the window. When Ken had told her that her mother had been moved to a hospice a week before that, it had been two weeks of discovering herself frozen and finding the minutes had disappeared.

The house her mother still owned but had not lived in since Harriet was a child was slightly uphill, on the border between Bronx and

Manhattan and cradled by trees. The Victorian home had become somewhat abandoned when her mother Linda could no longer muster the energy to restore it for sale. The money made from the sell would have gone to pay medical bills, but even as Linda, Ken and her daughter touched up paint on the crown molding and replaced fogged glass panes in the downstairs bedroom, they all knew a nearly million dollar home far the epicenter of the city and in the middle of a recession would be difficult to unload on anyone.

The air in the house was stale. Dust modes floated down the green-tinted shafts of light from the stained-glass-covered dark wood door. Ken opened the front-facing bay windows, letting in the chilly September air. Harriet placed the urn on the coffee table and pushed her hands into her coat pockets.

"Do you want anything to eat?" Ken said as he strode over to her, placing his hand on the small of her back.

Harriet didn't respond, she wasn't paying attention. Instead, she walked over to the tarp-covered armchair and pulled it off in a few jerky tugs.

"She loved this chair. She would watch Cheers and drink hot cocoa. It didn't matter if it was winter or not,"

"Do you want to keep it?" Ken said, looking around the living room.

Harriet shook her head no and ran her fingers over the small hand-embroidered birds of paradise. "There's a few credit card bills I didn't know about. She had a few loans from Citibank to restore the house. Apparently shingling the turrets was very expensive and the new stained glass in the bay windows at the back of the house..." she trailed off and moved closer to Ken, feeling his breath on the top of her head. Racking up credit card debt was just like her mother. She was thankful it was in her mother's own name and not in her name like her father had done when Harriet turned 18. He used it to get a statue for the backyard, thinking it would help sell the house. He began to pay it off but the payments stopped after four months.

If Harriet could have her way, she would keep the armchair, the box of marbles locked in a box the in attic, and the house but she could not bring herself to take Ken on his offer. The weight on her chest was too great and with the financial burden lifted she could buy new things. They would never amount to the old things and never fill her heart as fully but it would appease Ken to know she was making strides to move forward. He had been worried about her. He always worried about her.

Ken said, "I'm going to turn on the heat," as he walked away. Harriet took that moment to loosen her coat and let her stomach breathe. The zippers and the non-stretching wool material of the coat could not have been good for the baby. The bump was mostly her own fat, if she were being honest with herself, as the little human was no bigger than a kidney bean. Knowing she was carrying a child was what made her focus on remaining calm, though most times it didn't work. Most of the time she found herself under the covers with the calculator on her phone trying to soften the blow of all the numbers and percentages that spun in her head when she dreamed. The clatter of the heat turning on made Harriet readjust for Ken's arrival. She pulled out her white blouse to accommodate her small bump.

"There's some boxes filled with records and books Mr. Douglass dropped off."

Mr. Douglass was Harriet's former neighbor before they moved into an apartment in midtown. The relationship between her mom and father was beyond strained and it became explosive. If her mom did not move out, then her dad would have. Mr. Douglass had a son named Joshua around her age and they were friends until they had an argument over politics. Joshua was sexist, a trait he picked up from the guys at his school.

The box was soggy at the bottom and packed tight with 7-inch vinyl. The edges of the record covers where thin white tattered lines. The most used were in the middle. Some were shrink-wrapped. Harriet slid a worn record out of the box, pinching it with the fingers to get a hold. It was an beige and titled *Post Marked Stamps* with a small heart shaped stamp and a etched pine tree standing lonely at the bottom. On the other side was a framed picture of two young black-haired girls sitting shoulder to shoulder, their eyes blank. The first listed was *Black in the Eye* by Aspera Ad Astra. Harriet remembered when her mom bought the album from a dusty record store one year ago on a whim. The hair salon was full so they walked around to kill some time, linking arms and talking about their disappointment that *Cane* ended after only one season. The record was in perfect condition but packed haphazardly inside of a Rubbermaid bin marked $10 for 2 and $15 for 3. The cashier smelled of chewing Tabaco and something sharp. Harriet's mother asked "What's your opinion on this?" over her shoulder and he responded, "It's from the Psychedelphia scene, you like you're old enough to have seen the original thing so I don't know if you'll like it." Harriet automatically registered the insult but her mother did seem to and instead flipped over the record and read the list of songs "*Post from Disorder...Belated Blues...Nagarkot...Pincushion.*" Harriet, unable to help herself Googled Nagarkot, it was a small village in Nepal. The books were cheap pharmacy romance novels, some with the movie poster as the cover. Many of the pages were dog-eared in her copy of *Room*. Harriet bought that book for her on a whim, feeling it would be disrespectful to visit her in the hospital empty handed. Linda was in bed receiving an IV because she was very dehydrated. The chemo made drinking and eating difficult for Linda.

"Hm," Harriet said, rubbing her pants legs with the tips of her fingers. Ken knew that pose too well. Harriet had a habit of folding inward with her feet close together and standing too still when she had second thoughts or wasn't sure how to say what she needed to say. Harriet stood the same way at Mount Sinai Hospital when her mother said she had decided to not go through chemotherapy.

"What do you need?" Ken said, walking closer to her side.

"I want to look around," Harriet said " before we start to talk about selling."

Ken took her hand and they walked through the archway leading to the small library. Built into the wall were ceiling-high bookshelves and case-wrapped and leather-bound volumes of poetry and literature. The most worn and loved copies sat on the lowest shelf. Her memories of the room were faint, but she could still smell the hot cider that was brought out on Christmas. "Every year mom would put up posters for a Christmas day reading of *A Christmas Carol*. Dad was always worried she'd attract crazies from the street but a lot of kids and their parent's came. Some would bring food. It was always the best," Harriet said.

Tears slipped down her cheeks and she wiped them away quickly.

"Mom has a few first editions. We can start with that," She walked to the bookcase on the left. Her mother loved Dracula. She had brought Harriet along for a last-minute vacation in the middle of October to take her to Wahpeton, North Dakota because an old woman had a mint-condition 1st edition copy. The town looked like it belonged in the old west with two long blocks facing each other—the nucleus of their existence. The red Childcraft encyclopedias would be the first on her hit list, the memories of 3rd grade science reports giving her hand a phantom cramp. Harriet's dad helped with homework but the memories always caused a twinge of anxiety. He stood over her, mostly pointing at the things she spelt and computed wrong. Harriet rubbed holes into her paper and when the exhaustion would set in she would achieve a more incorrect answer.

"Hey." Ken said. "We don't have to do this today or even this month…"

Harriet wanted to get rid of things. She also wanted to keep things. Her rational mind also knew each penny mattered a lot and each copper disk would free Ken and her from the debt prison they now resided in. She was not worried about money until her mother became ill. At Hunter College, where she'd met Ken, it surprised her that some of her classmates couldn't afford lunch everyday or they needed to take out loans to afford the measly 5k tuition. Ken was one of these classmates, but he didn't worry as much. He was careful about money and only once did he bring up her wealth.

It was during their senior year in the middle of November when Linda told Harriet she wasn't going through with chemo. Ken looked livid when Harriet told him in the waiting room and he said couldn't understand why Linda would not spend money she had. Harriet didn't have an answer and mirrored some of his anger, even going as far as to ignore her mother's calls for a couple days. Latter she scoffed when her mother's doctor said she had a treatment plan, as if no treatment was treatment at all. Harriet now cringed at these memories. The rain started up again and poured down on the unkempt shrubs in the backyard and further drowned the Kentucky grass.

Ken led her away from the books. The next stop on their tour was the study through the second archway via the library. It was empty due to the resurfacing they had started but didn't finish four months ago. The floor was still covered with white and circular scuffmarks and small ridges of dust. Upstairs was her mother's favorite room. The large, scalloped bargeboards were very noticeable and triangulated any sunlight. Cream-colored embossed wallpaper covered the walls and a closet covered in hand-painted slivery koi fish that seemed to circle and swim underneath the surface. Ken looked at the closet for a while, and his finger hovered over a delicately painted koi, unsure if he should touch it. Her mother wouldn't have minded it. As a child, Harriet watched her mother paint and draw and then she would suddenly take up tiny Harriet and have her feel and experiment with the materials. Linda always advised to be careful but Harriet was allowed to feel with her fingers the differing textures of oil, tempera, and acrylic and watched the ripples formed by the addition of water to watercolor paint. Linda thought that through the multi-sensory experience of art that Harriet would develop artistic ability.

"She would have let you touch it," Harriet said.

"It's too perfect, your mother was very talented."

Harriet wanted to add 'our mom,' and though it wasn't official, her mother had considered Ken part of the family and nudged Harriet to get him to propose. She would often ask how he was doing and if he had plans for the weekend, things she would have never asked any of Harriet's past boyfriends. People her mother didn't like weren't invited to brunch or church and certainly weren't allowed in the family Christmas photo for the family Christmas card. Harriet wondered if Ken noticed the special treatment or if he thought it was how her mother treated all of her boyfriends. Ken was always there for both of them and would rub against her mother's conservative political views, but though it irritated her Linda told Harriet she preferred his honesty. Other boyfriends laughed at all of her mother's corny jokes. Ken only laughed when it was funny and if it were especially bad, he would tease her.

Ken, unlike Harriet, understood sooner why her mother chose to forego treatment and was not as fazed by Linda's dark humor or the small wishes she made before her health quickly plummeted. The one that made Harriet most uncomfortable was the going away party. The cake and the candy and ridiculous amounts of food she shouldn't have been eating made her dizzy and depressed, but Linda didn't notice Harriet's mood and enjoyed herself. Friends and neighbors talked for a week afterward. Some of the gossip was kind, and the other and more conservative side took offense and called the party morbid. Many things about the last few months were morbid but loyalty wasn't something either Harriet or Ken took lightly.

Linda had been sick for a few months before she had been diagnosed. It started last summer. It began as an occasional stomachache and neither Harriet nor her father thought much of it. When Harriet's father died months later from a heart attack Linda began to have difficultly eating and keeping food down. Both Harriet and Ken first attributed the loss of appetite to stress due to her father's passing. Though Harriet knew how strained their relationship was it was not impossible that she felt loss. Perhaps even angry of not having the last word after everything he had put them both through. When Linda would go a day without eating and claim she was full, that was when Harriet made Linda go to the hospital. The waiting room was softly lit and the deep blue Saxony carpet looked like a placid lake. Harriet wished she melt into it and be sucked deep down into it tightly packed crevices. Ken placed his hand on top of hers, making her right palm sweaty. Her mother didn't look worried, but Harriet noticed how frail-looking her mother's hands were and how a mild breeze would make her shiver. She looked even weaker when she stood, her center of gravity seeming to have shifted onto her left leg.

Hearing from her mother's doctor that she had stage 1 stomach cancer was at first a bit of a relief. She thought, "they'll just remove it, she'll have some chemo and life will proceed as normal," but it was immediately shattered when she said she didn't want chemo and the doctor told them about the possibility of it spreading. It was like being punched in the chest, hearing her mother was going to slowly die. Harriet watched Linda arrange herself as if she planned to leave immediately. She shuffled through business cards as if she had something she was retrieving for the doctor. The doctor's eyes were slightly downcast as he spoke as he toyed with his blue and yellow *Cymbalta* pen.

After the appointment, Linda talked to Harriet as if she had not gotten the most horrifying news of her life. Linda dragged them into the gift shop. She bought water and shakily set a dollar and two quarters into the hand of the florist that was filling in, leaving a bouquet of lilies incomplete, the cellophane wrapping unsecured with ribbon. Ken lumbered beside both of them, his face red and lips pressed into thin pink lines. The first thing Linda talked about was the house and about finishing the renovations. The house was not lived in for six years since her father moved out. Renovations were started when Harriet was five but they were often left incomplete, a habit her father hated and often fought with her mother about. Harriet's father also said the renovations were hobbies, no matter how ambition and/or dangerous they were.

In the car Linda told Harriet to take her to Lowe's so she could buy nails. Harriet missed the exit twice, her hands shaking, veering the wheels just slightly to the right, and eyes watery. The cold air of the store temporarily moved her focus from her sadness to her pink chapped hands. Linda was offered help by a bored-looking old man wearing pants that were a size too big, but she didn't need any help. She went to the hand-held tool aisle and filled the cart with a few boxes of 3 2/3 nails and 7-inch nails she told Harriet over her shoulder would be for the new door. Ken helped Linda shop, looking less upset than Harriet. In another aisle, as he was standing next to Linda putting an order in for tile, he texted Harriet that she should help her mom. Harriet stuffed the phone deep down inside her red wool coat and wandered around aimlessly until she found an empty aisle to let some tears flow.

They walked around the house a bit more, passing by one disheveled room after another and some rooms covered in tarp or large plastic buckets and bags of debris before pausing at Harriet's childhood room. It was empty with the exception of an empty cradle, a bookcase, and a pallet of cherry wood to redo the floors.

"I don't think it's safe to be in this room without a mask, it's not good for you," Ken said. He hesitated a bit at the end and it made her more self-conscious. Harriet readjusted her shirt. She eyed the walnut cradle in the corner. The rockers were scuffed but with a small bottle of wood polish and some paint it would look like new. There was a slight crack near the heart shaped cutouts on the end. Harriet was told when she was six her cousin became over excited rocked the cradle too hard, tipping on its' side with her inside when she was a baby. It was why she had small fleshy scar on her knee. Harriet's phone buzzed in her back pocket and she checked her notifications. The real estate agent had sent a long-winded e-mail stating she could not take on the house due to it still being in the process of being restored and the fact it was on the market for close to eight years. Though she had expected, this Harriet wanted to cry.

"He doesn't think he can sell it. It's all about making a commission these days."

"Please Harriet, don't cry. It's only been two weeks of trying. That's no time," Ken said, grabbing Harriet in his arms. Harriet pulled away a moment later, not wanting to cry anymore and worry him.

"Hey, I'm fine," Harriet said "We can start talking about it now. I've got the papers and we can call to other places," Harriet said. Her eyes stung and her olive cheeks were hot.

Nonetheless, Harriet walked out the room and Ken had to take larger strides to keep up with her as she walked to the kitchen. It was the only room in the house that was completely renovated. The silver appliances and metal kitchen island clashed with the antiquated furnishings and overall dim quality of the lights throughout the house. Ken placed the statements and bills and the stack of folders on the kitchen island. They sorted them a week ago by origin, the only act they were emotionally able to do at that point.

"Did you have any realtors in mind?"

"He sold luxury properties so we have to find some place similar. Close to a million dollars was put into this house. I don't understand why he can't try."

"Maybe he's intimidated," Ken said, flipping through bills.

"Maybe we're sitting on something worthless to the rest of the world," Harriet said, her cheek resting on her hand. The feeling of nausea washed over her again, and she jumped down from the stool, nearly taking it with her. In a gasping and jerky motion she vomited into the sink. She washed out her mouth as Ken stood beside her, his hand rubbing her back.

"Harriet" Ken said. "Are you pregnant?"

Harriet stood, her hands clawed on the sink to keep her balance, and half-shook her head as she strained to not cry.

"We can't afford a baby," Harriet whispered down into the sink.
"If we sell the house—"
"This house is a wreck," Harriet said.
"We sell our house and live here, we'll have just enough to pay down more than half of the debt," Ken said, stroking his hand through her long wavy hair.
"You've thought about this. Why didn't you tell me?" Harriet's' light brown eyes were narrow and accusatory.
"I didn't want to accuse you of being pregnant because you ate half my food." Harriet laughed and a smile struggled to break across her tear-streaked cheeks.
"I can't have anything to myself," Harriet muttered under her breath "it's not fair."
"How do you think I feel?" Ken said "I've been starving for days now. Everyone in the house got to eat but me." He led her back to the table and grabbed her small hands in his, kissing them.
He said nothing for a few moments and what plagued his mind was if Harriet would really keep the baby and if she thought it was worth the struggle. They were not married and had a limited amount of money. All of Harriet's inheritance had gone to a year of chemo in a last minute effort to save Linda's life. It bought them valuable time but watching how quickly she had deteriorated from that point on was horrible.
"I love you, Harriet," Ken said. He meant all of her and that included the budding life inside her. He feared with all his being of losing another life and he could feel all her fear though her trembling hands.
"I love you," Harriet said, her voice breathless.
The rain had stopped but rainwater continued to drip down the turrets and from the gutters. There was no sun, but only a hazy mist that blanketed the streets.

# About the Author

A. L. Young is a New Yorker, born and raised. Her beloved genres are dystopia and fantastic fiction. She is an alumna of Sweet Briar College. When she isn't writing, she's taking walks through Central Park and rewatching *Criminal Minds*.

## Also by A. L. Young

The Half-Blessed

Made in the USA
Middletown, DE
21 June 2024